MY CAT IS **WEIRD,**

HE DOES **STRANGE** THINGS.

HE POOPS IN BOXES...
CENSORED

AND PLAYS WITH STRINGS!

AND WHEN I'M **ASLEEP,**

HE PLAYS AND **SINGS.**

WHEN I'M AWAKE AND HAVING **FUN,**

HE'S SOUND
ASLEEP IN THE SUN!

HE
SCRATCHES
RUGS...

AND
EATS UP
BUGS...

AND NEVER LIKES
HIS **BELLY RUBBED!!!**

HE SLEEPS UP HIGH!

HE
SLEEPS
DOWN LOW!

WHEN I'M ASLEEP
HE **BITES** MY TOES!

MY CAT IS WEIRD AND THAT'S A FACT...
10

HE HIDES IN CORNERS AND THEN ATTACKS!!!

MY CAT IS WEIRD AND
THIS IS TRUE,

BUT I'D NEVER TRADE HIM,
NOT EVEN TO YOU!!!